For my boys: Jackson, Tucker, and Walker
This book is my letter to you. Love the world. Embrace it. Be kind. Be brave.
And don't be afraid to change it. Love always, Mom

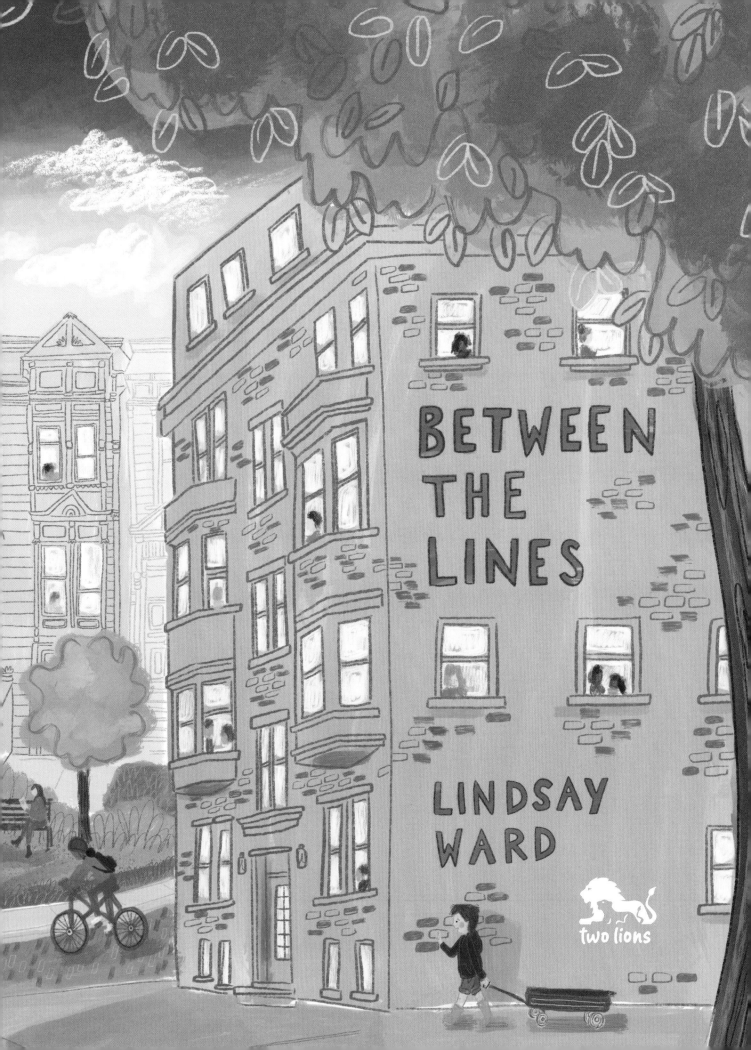

I was just a boy when the colors were swept from our street.

The sounds became quieter.
Everyone was too busy
to notice we were fading.

Then one night the sky cracked wide open.
Lightning crashed while wind thundered through
narrow alleys.

Rain poured down, deep into the darkness.

We stood in silence.

When our sounds did return, they were different.
Questions filled the spaces in between.

WHERE HAD
WOULD IT

THE COLOR GONE?

COME BACK?

Lines were drawn.

Our street filled with . . .

an empty sadness.

Days turned into weeks.
And then a month.
Then a year.

Nothing was fixed. Most people got used to it.
Forgetting that we had once been so full of color...

. . . rust redbrick roads bathed in ripe, orange mornings.
Lemon Popsicle yellow melting, sticky and sweet.
Freshly cut green against bluebird skies.
And a sea of stars sprinkled on velvet purple nights.

Every night
I dreamt about our colors.

When I awoke, I searched and searched. . . .

In cracks and slivers, in gaps and rifts.

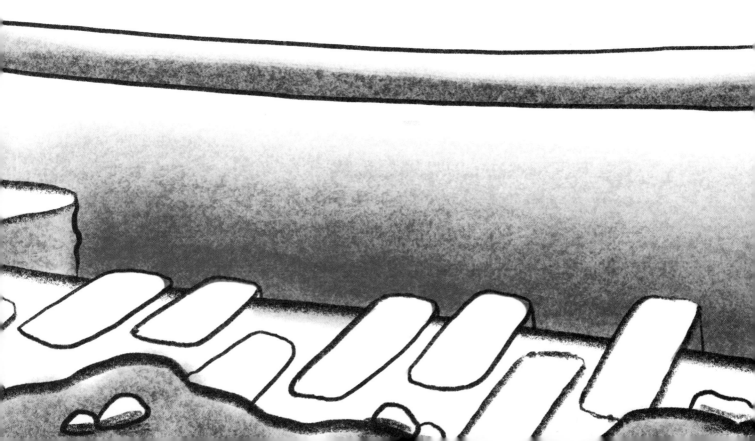

But there was nothing left between the lines.

Then one night I didn't dream at all.
I'd forgotten the colors.

WHAT IF I NEVER SAW THEM AGAIN?

There was only one thing left to do....

We were finally working together when suddenly the rains returned. Stronger than ever.

The storm's fury lit the sky.
A loud crash stole the lights,
covering us in a blanket of night.

Together we stood, quietly huddled in darkness.
Eyes wide against windows wet.

And then . . .

. . . a whisper.

A smile.

A laugh burst from the dark.

Once we started we couldn't stop.

The sounds of our street filled the room, just like before,
when the color had been rich, and full, and everywhere.
In the dawn light we held steady.

Together we had survived the storm.
The sun peeked out, lighting the whole neighborhood.

Voices big and small flooded the street in celebration.
Laughter and love spilled out . . .

...filling the space between the lines.